NOT ME!

Nicola Killen

EGMONT

With big thanks to my classmates, tutors, friends and family.
N. K.

Jake   Jane   Bertie

NOT ME!

Nicola Killen

Paul   Louise   Jess the Pup

Who's been

eating
all the cake?

NOT
ME!

said
Jake.

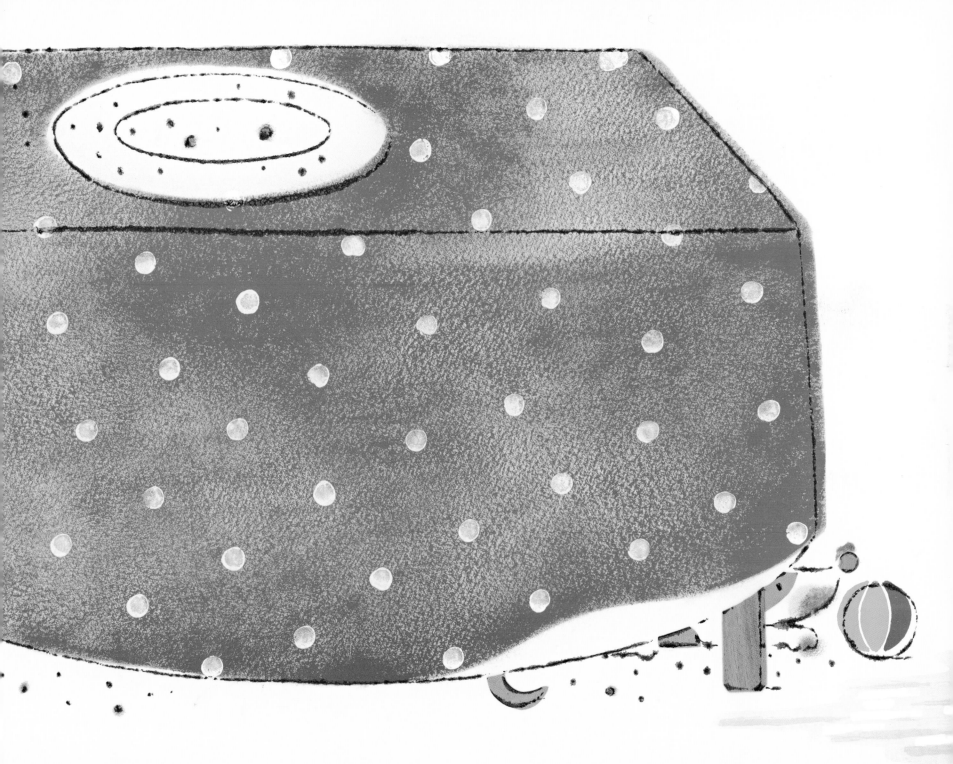

Who's been

playing in

the rain?

NOT me!

said Jane.

Who's been
MAKING
the carpet dirty?

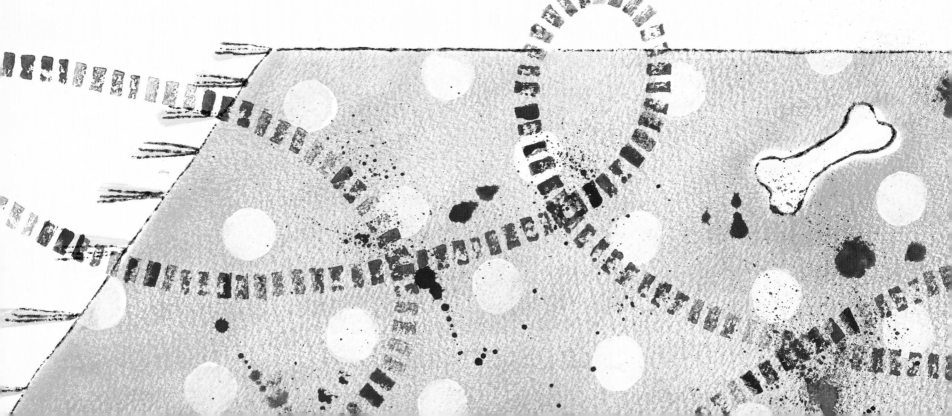

NOT ME!

said Bertie.

Who's been LEAVING ...?

hand prints on the wall?

NOT me!

said Paul.

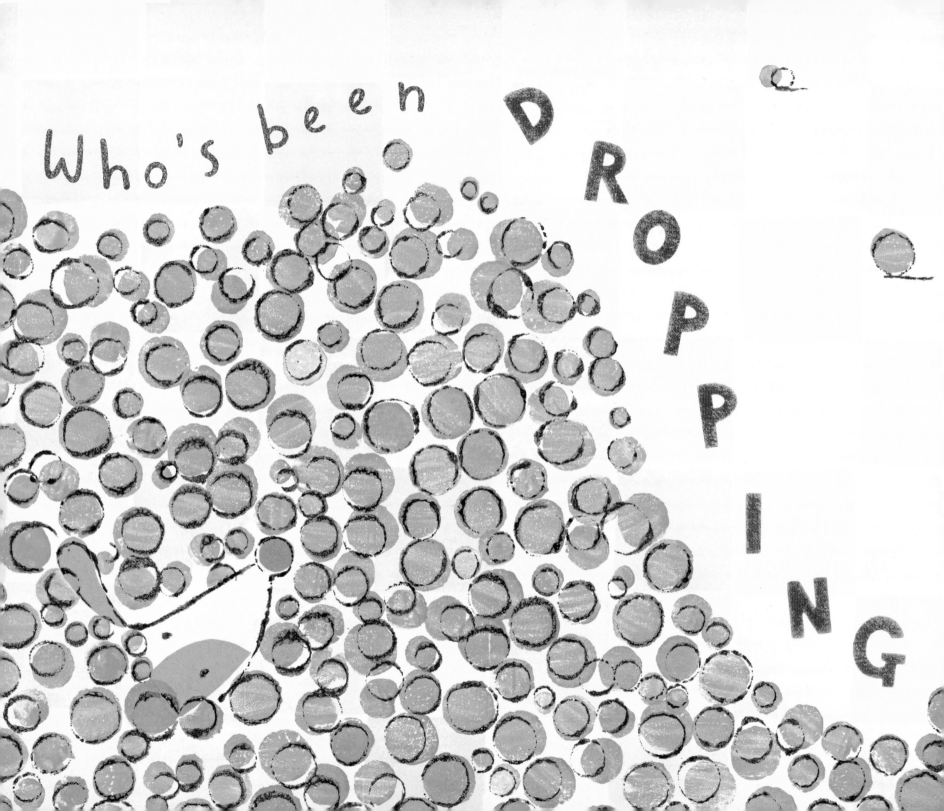

all these peas?

Not Me! said Louise.

So who's been making all this MESS?

CAN'T YOU GUESS?!

But who's

going to CLEAN and TIDY UP?

NOT ME!

thought Tess the Pup.

First published in Great Britain 2010
by Egmont UK Limited
239 Kensington High Street
London W8 6SA

Text and illustrations copyright © Nicola Killen 2010

The moral rights of the author/illustrator have been asserted

ISBN 978 1 4052 4829 7 (Hardback)
ISBN 978 1 4052 4830 3 (Paperback)

1 3 5 7 9 10 8 6 4 2

A CIP catalogue record for this title
is available from the British Library

Printed and bound in Singapore

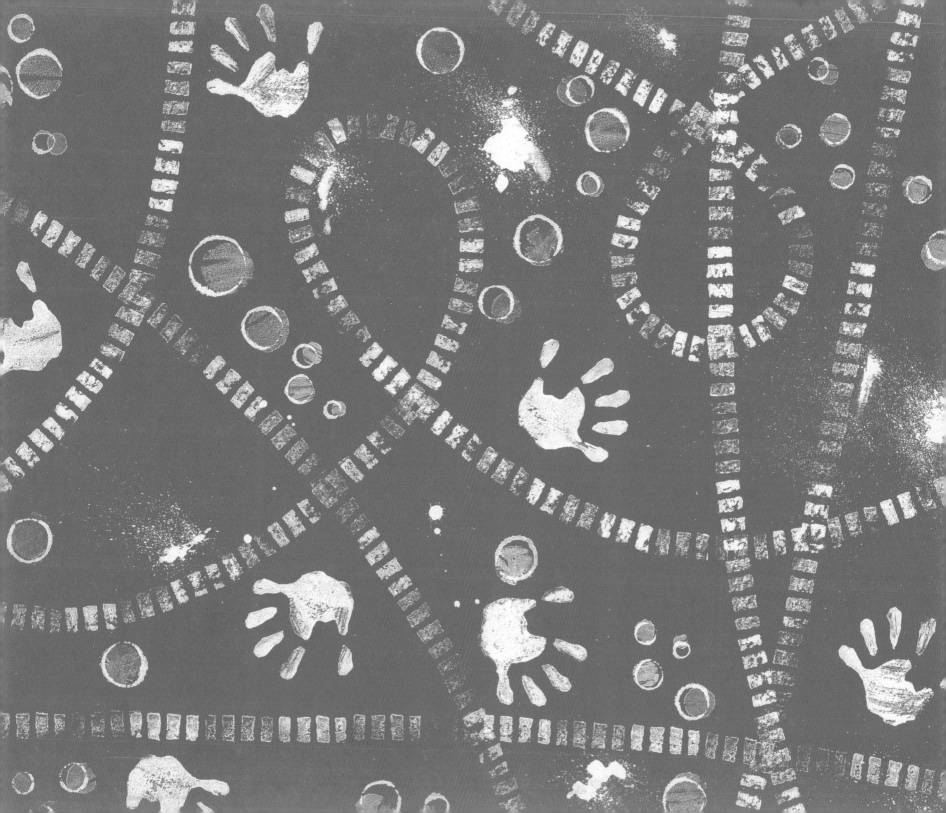